Jaco the Leek

CAT WEATHERILL

Illustrated by Brett Breckon

To Max
Best Wishes,
Cat Weatherill
x

Pont

Published in 2008 by Pont Books, an imprint of
Gomer Press, Llandysul, Ceredigion, SA44 4JL

ISBN 978 1 84323 913 0

A CIP record for this title is available from the British Library.

This book is published with the financial support of the
Welsh Books Council.

Printed and bound in Wales at
Gomer Press, Llandysul, Ceredigion

Contents

Chapter 1

A Wish at Bedtime

This is me, Cai.

And this is my older brother, Jaco. His real name is Jac Owain Evans, but everyone calls him Jaco. Even the teachers sometimes, though never when they're telling him off.

This is a leek.

And this is Saint David. He's not in the story. He's dead. He died a very long time ago. But he is special to the people of Wales. So special, he has his very own day,

7

Saint David's Day. It's on the same date every year, the first of March, and everyone uses it to celebrate being Welsh. Some people wear daffodils pinned to their jackets. Some people wear *leeks*. They must be mad! Leeks are stinky old things.

There are concerts and parties all over Wales. In our school everyone dresses up in Welsh costume.

That's what usually goes on. But last year was different. Last year, my brother wanted to do something extra-special for Saint David's Day. He decided to be a leek. He didn't want to *dress up* as a leek. No. That wasn't enough for Jaco. He wanted to BE a leek. So he made a wish and it came true. And this is how it happened.

The story begins the night before Saint David's Day. Jaco and I are lying in our beds, side by side like a pair of slippers. Listening to the rain falling *tip-a-tip-a-tip-a* on the roof when Jaco says: 'Do you believe in the Tooth Fairy?'

'No,' I say. 'She's not real.'

'I'm not so sure,' says Jaco. 'I hope she *is* real, because I want her to grant me a wish tonight.'

He gets out of bed, goes to the wardrobe and pulls out his special box. I hear him feeling for something in the dark. Then he puts the box back and climbs into bed again.

'I've been saving my last tooth,' he says, 'but I think the time has come to use it.'

'OK,' I say, playing along. 'What are you going to wish for?'

'Something special for Saint David's Day. I'm tired of dressing up.'

I know how he feels. I haven't made a costume this year. I'm just going to wear my rugby shirt. But Jaco usually makes a big effort. He loves to be the best.

'This year,' he says, 'I want to be a leek.'

'You can't start making a costume now. It's gone ten o'clock.'

'No, I don't want a costume. I want to *be* a leek!' There's real excitement in his voice. 'I'm putting the tooth under my pillow, see? Now

9

I'll make the wish.' He takes a deep breath. 'Tooth Fairy. If you are listening . . . please turn me into a leek for Saint David's Day.'

Nothing happens.

I hear Jaco sigh. I'm disappointed too. I wanted a flash of lightning or something. I turn over in bed. 'Sleep tight,' I say. 'Sorry your wish didn't come true.'

But I'm wrong to say that, because the wish *does* come true! There must be a Tooth Fairy and she must
be listening. Because
the very next morning,
Saint David's Day, the
tooth has gone and my
brother Jaco is a leek.

Chapter 2

Jaco the Leek

I wake up and there's a strange smell in the room. Not old socks or stinky trainers – something else. I open my eyes. The curtains are drawn, but there is a tiny bit of light to see by. I sit up, look around and *AARGH!* Where's our Jaco gone? There's a huge great THING in his bed, half-under the duvet. I want to know what it is, but I'm terrified to look. What if it grabs me, as soon as I get close? It could be a monster. A terrible beast with fangs and claws and poisonous stingers.

Light. I need more light.

Carefully . . . quietly . . . very, very slowly, I get out of bed. I creep to the window, keeping one eye on the horrible Thing, and pull the curtains back. Sunshine pours into the room and it's Jaco! He's turned into a leek!

He does a big, sleepy yawn. I stand there, just staring at him. Jaco is *enormous*. His

head has gone. He has no shoulders, no neck – just a face and ears sticking out of a bright white body. I pull the duvet back. He is so *long!* Much taller than he usually is. He still has arms, but he has no legs – just that long, thin, white body with a pair of feet sticking out the end.

'It worked!' he cries. He grins, and he looks like the man in the moon. He's so pale, it's scary. As for his hair, he seems to have a palm tree growing out of the top of his head.

'Help me get up,' he says. 'I want to look in the mirror.'

'How?' I ask. Jaco is lying flat on his back. I don't know what to do.

'Take hold of my hands,' he suggests. 'Pull.'

I try that, but it doesn't work. His body is so stiff – no bendiness to him at all. I'm scared of snapping him. 'I'll have to get Mam,' I say, and I run downstairs to the kitchen.

Mam is making porridge when I burst in. She has the phone glued to her ear. I know it will be her best friend, Gwen.

'*Never!*' says Mam. A grin comes to her

face, big as a banana. 'She never did. In front of *everyone?*'

'Mam,' I say, though I know she won't hear me. 'Mam!'

'Never on this earth!' she squeals.

'Mam!'

'What, love?' She's putting bread in the toaster now.

'Jaco can't get out of bed.'

'Hold on,' she says into the phone. She goes to the bottom of the stairs.

'JACO!' She shouts so loud, the windows rattle. Not just in the house – right down our street.

'GET YOUR LAZY BACKSIDE DOWN THESE STAIRS NOW!'

She stomps back into the kitchen. 'Sorry about that,' she says into the phone. 'Our Jaco won't get out of bed again.'

The toast launches itself out of the toaster. Mam catches it with one hand. I am so impressed, I forget why I'm there. Then I remember. I tug at her sleeve.

'No,' I say. 'Jaco *wants* to get out of bed but he can't.'

Mam frowns. 'I'll call you back, Gwen,' she says into the phone. 'Seems our Jaco's lost the use of his legs this morning.'

I'm dying to tell her – I love it when Mam howls – but I want her to see for herself.

She huffs and puffs up the stairs like the big, bad wolf. She's not built for climbing, our mam. She's built for cuddles – that's what she tells us. If Dad's there when she says it, she winks at him. He goes pink and hides behind his gardening magazine.

He's funny, our dad. We don't have a garden.

'Aieeee!'

Mam has seen Jaco.

'What's this, boy? Who's done this to you?'

Mam is gearing up for a fight. Take on Jaco and you get Mam too.

'It's all right, Mam!' says Jaco. He's lying on the bed like a rolled-up carpet. 'I asked the Tooth Fairy to do it.'

'*Why?*'

'For Saint David's Day. I'm sick of dressing up as a sheep.'

Mam shakes her head. 'You don't think you're going into school like *that?*'

'Of course I am!' says Jaco. 'That's why I've done it! And I've got a match today. Wood Green Juniors. I have to be there.'

'You've got no legs,' says Mam. Like he didn't know. 'How are you going to run?'

'I've got feet,' says Jaco.

'I've got fingers,' says Mam, 'but I can't play the piano.'

'I've got big ears,' I say, 'but I'm not an elephant.'

Jaco glares at me. 'You've got a mouth,' he snaps, 'but you don't have a brain.'

He's getting worried now. I can tell.

'I need to get out of bed, Mam,' he says. 'You're right – I don't know what I can do yet.'

Mam turns to me. 'You take his feet, Cai, and swing them off the bed. I'll pull him up from this end.'

I grab Jaco's ankles and drag him round. Mam seizes hold of his hands and pulls with all her strength. Oh, it's hard work! Jaco can't bend in the middle and he's really heavy. Solid leek. It's like lifting a tree. But we do it.

'Right,' says Mam. 'I'll finish making breakfast. Cai, you get dressed then help your brother downstairs. Once you've eaten, you can both get off to school. But you must stay with him all day, Cai. You understand? He'll need you to look after him.'

Mam goes downstairs. I throw on some clothes and start to follow but Jaco holds me back.

'Wait!' he hisses. 'I can't go to school like this. I've got no pants on!'

'You don't need pants,' I tell him. 'Not today.'

'I can't go without pants,' he says. 'I'm shy.'

Shy? Jaco? I don't think so. When we went on a trip to the zoo, Jaco showed his bottom to a cage full of monkeys. Mrs Williams saw him do it. The *whole school* saw him do it. He didn't care. Mrs Williams told him off. They started it, he said, and he was right. They did. Monkeys can be very rude when they don't like you.

So Jaco – shy? No. But he hands me his pants – his best, stripy underpants – and wants me to dress him.

'How?' I say. I hold them up. Show him the two legs.

'Easy,' says Jaco. 'Open one leg really wide, hold it down on the ground and I'll jump in.'

I can't believe it will work, but it does. Jaco is *always* right. Of course, with only one pant leg filled, the other one is flapping empty. But Jaco has a plan for that too. He gets me to fetch a belt and wrap the empty leg behind him. Then he fastens the buckle.

'Perfect!' he says – and it is. He has the body of a leek. He is wearing nothing but a pair of underpants and an 'I ♥ Wales' belt, but Jaco looks cool. Anyone else would look as mad as a moonboy, but not my brother. I have to smile.

Jaco grins back and puts his hand in the air, like he's flying. 'Look out, world!' he cries. 'Here comes *JACO THE LEEK!*'

Chapter 3

The Good Shepherd

So Jaco and I walk to school. I have to help
him put on his trainers first. He can't go to
school with bare feet. 'That would look silly,'
he says. Having the body of a leek, of course,
isn't silly. Not to Jaco.

As we walk down the street, people turn to
look. They point and smile and laugh. They all
think Jaco is dressed up. I can understand why.
From a distance, it just looks like a very clever
costume.

Jaco loves the attention. He grins and waves.
Winks at the girls. And he's so busy playing the
star, he doesn't see the kerb before it's too late.
Doomf! He goes down like a bowling pin. So
now he's lying there, splatted in the gutter.

'Jaco!' I roll him onto his back. 'Jaco! Are
you all right? Are you hurt?'

'Get me up,' he says through tight teeth.
'Get me up!'

People are watching. He's starting to go pink. Not just in his cheeks – all over. Bright girly pink. He looks like a stick of rock. And just for a moment, I wonder what he would look like inside, if you cut him in two. Would he have his name running all the way through him? *Jaaaaacooooooo!*

'*Get me up,*' he growls. '*Come on, turnip-brain!*'

'Excuse me,' I say. 'I don't deserve that. I haven't done anything wrong.'

'You were supposed to be looking after me.'

I let him stay there. Jaco starts kicking his feet. He's rocking like a beetle on its back. It's very funny.

Jaco gives in. 'Please,' he begs. 'Everyone's watching. And I'm starting to feel a bit . . . *faint.*' His arms flop, his head rolls back and he looks really bad. I begin to panic.

'No! Wait! Hang on! I'll get you up. Don't die. Please! Mam will kill me!'

I grab his hands and start to pull, but he is way too heavy for me. Then I see Ethan Lloyd coming down the road dressed as a shepherd.

He has a tea towel round his head, his mam's sandals on his feet and his sister's nightie covering the rest of him.

'Cool costume,' he says when he reaches us. Then he just stands there, watching me struggling.

'Give us a hand,' I say. 'I'm trying to get him up.'

'You should have asked, boy,' says Ethan, joining in. With a grunt and heave and a *one-two-three-HUP!* the job is done.

'Flamin' firecrackers,' he says, rubbing his back. 'That was like lifting a baby hippopotamus. What's this costume made of? Rubber?' Ethan pinches Jaco's skin with his grubby fingers.

'Ow!' squeals Jaco. 'Gerroff! It's not a costume, it's me. I've turned into a leek.'

Ethan's eyes widen. 'What – *forever?*'

'No, you daft dollop. Just for today.'

'Oh, right,' says Ethan. 'I mean, you wouldn't want to stay like that forever, would you? You'd never be able to drive a Formula One racing car.'

Yeah. Like Jaco's planning to buy a racing car when he grows up. He won't get a Ford or a Toyota like normal people. He'll buy a whacking great Formula One Ferrari and drive it around the Valleys at 200 miles an hour. But he won't be able to fit Mam in it, so when they go to the supermarket, she'll have to go in a trailer on the back. I don't think so, Ethan.

'Anyway,' Jaco says to him as we reach the school gates. 'Why are you dressed like that?'

'I'm a shepherd, aren't I?' says Ethan. 'There are loads of shepherds in Wales. It's a real Welsh thing.'

'Yeah,' says Jaco, 'but you belong in Bethlehem, not Brynmawr. It's Saint David's Day, not the Christmas concert.'

Ethan grins. 'You're just jealous, boy!' he says and with that, he disappears into the crowded playground.

My mates start arriving. They have all made a big effort to wear something special. I start to feel under-dressed in a plain old rugby shirt. Angharad Rees is in full Welsh costume: long

skirt, shawl, black pointy hat, the lot. Tom Roberts is dressed as a coal miner, with a dirty face and a working lamp. Kristina Zaremba is a daffodil. She's in a long green dress, with an enormous yellow bonnet strapped to her head. It must have taken hours to make – and she isn't even Welsh. She's Polish. Her mam and dad work at the meat factory. But she loves Wales. Really, really loves it. And she speaks Welsh better than anyone in the class.

I'm a bit puzzled by Rhodri Taylor, though. He's dressed like a waiter. Black suit, white shirt and a black bow tie.

'I'm a singer,' he explains when I ask. 'Male voice choir.'

'Aah!' we all say at once. 'We get it now!'

'No,' says Kristina. 'I do not understand. Not everything. I know you are a singer – but why is there money *here*?'

She points. There is a ten pound note pinned to Rhodri's jacket. He shakes his head.

'I don't understand that either,' he confesses. 'My brother did it this morning. Said if I was going to be a singer, I had to be a tenner.'

'A *tenor*, Rhodri,' says Mrs Stephens, coming up behind us. 'It's a man who sings with a high voice rather than a low one.'

Rhodri scowls. 'I hate my brother,' he grumbles. 'He's always showing me up.'

Angharad and Kristina nod. 'Brothers are like that,' says Angharad.

How true, I think. Then I remember I'm supposed to be looking after mine. I turn around and he's gone.

'He's inside,' says Mrs Stephens. She must have seen the fright on my face. 'Look.'

Through the open door, I can see a green spiky head bobbing down the corridor.

'My mam wants me to stay with him,' I tell her. 'All day.'

'Then you had better come with me,' says Mrs Stephens, and we follow Jaco into the gloom of the junior school building.

Chapter 4

Stinko!

The bell has rung by the time Mrs Stephens and I reach the classroom. Everyone is in there, sitting down – except Jaco. He is standing behind his table at the back of the class.

'Sit down, Jaco,' says Mrs Stephens. 'We'll find a seat for your brother.'

'I can't, miss.'

'Sorry?' Mrs Stephens tilts her head to one side like an owl.

'I can't sit down, miss. I can't bend.'

'I see.' She smiles but she doesn't look friendly. Mrs Stephens doesn't like people messing around in class. She finds it hard to keep her temper. She looks cool on the outside, but inside she's a hot bubbling volcano. She can erupt at any time, with very little warning. And when she shouts, it's so loud, your ears flap like washing on a windy

26

day. 'I suggest you take the costume off,' she says.

'I can't, miss.'

'Oh, you *can*.' We hear the edge in her voice, sharp as a diamond dagger. 'You can put it on again later, when it's time for judging.'

'No, Mrs Stephens – really, I can't. It's not a costume.' Jaco turns to me for support. I nod furiously.

Mrs Stephens looks puzzled now. She moves closer to Jaco, gliding between the tables like an angry swan. Suddenly her nose begins to wrinkle.

'Jac Evans,' she says. 'You smell of onions.'

'Well – yes,' says Jaco. 'I'm a leek, miss. Part of the onion family.'

'Don't get clever with me,' says Mrs Stephens. 'You smell of onions. And I can't *stand* onions.'

'I don't think I smell that bad, miss. No more than a packet of cheese and onion crisps.'

'You do *not* smell like cheese and onion

crisps!' says Mrs Stephens, stamping her foot. 'I can *just about* bear the smell of cheese and onion crisps, but you *stink*.'

Oh! The whole class gasps at once. All the air gets sucked out of the room.

'Mrs Stephens was *rude!*' whispers Ellen Barton in horror. Ellen the Wet is Teacher's Pet. Ellen Barton worships Mrs Stephens and wants to be just like her when she grows up. Now she is in shock. She's gone as white as a candle.

'I was *not* rude, Ellen Barton,' snaps Mrs Stephens, rounding on her like a pit bull terrier. 'I was simply stating a fact. Telling the truth. And it *is* true. Jac Evans STINKS of onions. And *I CAN'T STAND THE SMELL OF ONIONS!*'

We believe her! We believe her! Every single one of us – every boy, every girl – even the guinea pig in the corner believes her. Ellen Barton believes her, though she is in tears now. We just want Mrs Stephens to calm down. We don't want her to blow her top. Not here. Not now. We're trapped. She'll go off like a Roman candle. Her head will go *BANG!* A fountain of

fire will fly from her body and we'll all be turned to dust. No – turned to stone, frozen in fear, like a room full of statues. And we'll all have horrible faces, with bug eyes and open mouths screaming Aaaargh!

Mrs Stephens starts pacing up and down the classroom, trying to get a grip on herself. She won't even look at Jaco now. 'Get out off my classroom,' she says quietly. Much too quietly for my liking. 'Get out of my classroom and stay out. I don't care where you go. I don't care what you do. Just *get out*.'

I grab hold of Jaco's arm and pull him towards the door. 'Don't say anything,' I plead. I know what Jaco's like. He never knows when to stop. 'Don't say *anything*.'

'Understood,' says Jaco. We escape through the door just in time. Behind us we hear the hammering of windows, loud as machine gun fire, as Mrs Stephens banishes the stink of Jaco from her room.

Chapter 5

Jaco the Souper H

Jaco and I wander towards the hall.

'I think she made a bit too much of it,' says Jaco. 'I don't smell that bad – do I?'

'You are a bit whiffy,' I say. 'But I'm getting used to it. And it's only for one day.'

'Exactly,' says Jaco.

So now we're in the hall, passing the kitchen, when we hear a wail.

'*Nooo!* You can't help me! No one can!'

Mrs Morgan, the Cook. It has to be. No one can make a fuss like Mrs Morgan. Mam went to school with her and says she was like that from Day One.

'There's no need to get angry with me, Mrs Morgan. I was only trying to help.' That's Mrs Williams, the Head.

'But you *can't* help,' wails Mrs Morgan, 'and I really wanted the children to have it.'

Now we're curious. What did Mrs Morgan

us to have? We hide behind the hall curtains and wait until Mrs Williams has gone. Then we go into the kitchen.

'*AIEEE!*' Mrs Morgan screams when she sees Jaco. 'What the – ?' She peers closer. 'It's Jaco Evans, isn't it? Oh my poor heart. I thought the aliens had landed. Little green men from Mars.'

We smile, but she's thumping her chest like her heart has stopped. *Making a show,* Mam would say.

'What did you mean, Mrs Morgan?' I ask. 'We heard you talking to Mrs Williams and you said you wanted the children to have it.'

'Leek soup!' she replies. 'I wanted you all to have leek soup for lunch. I make it special, just like my mam. But I need leeks and Dai the Veg has let me down.'

Dai the Veg isn't a cabbage or a carrot. He is a man who sells vegetables to the school. He drives a van called *The Green Machine* but it's yellow – just like Dai's teeth. I don't think Dai eats vegetables, just burgers and chips. I've seen the empty boxes in his van.

'I made the order last week,' says Mrs Morgan. 'But he turns up today empty-handed. *I'm sorry,* he says. *I've run out.* Run out! On Saint David's Day! Silly, *silly* man.'

'I can help,' says Jaco. 'You can have my top bits.'

Mrs Morgan smiles. 'I don't think so, love. It's a kind thought, but cardboard and green paint would make a very strange soup.'

'No,' says Jaco. 'This is all real. Feel.'

He leans forward. Mrs Morgan strokes his long green spiky hair with her fingers. 'You're right!' she says. 'It *is* real. Brilliant! It's not perfect – when you cook leeks, you use the long white stem, not the green leaves. But no one will taste the difference.'

And with that, she goes to a drawer, pulls out an ENORMOUS kitchen knife and runs straight at Jaco.

'NO-O-O-O-O!'

Jaco tries to run away backwards but he trips over his own feet. He crashes to the floor and there's Mrs Morgan standing over

him, knife in hand. It's like a horror movie.
It's fantastic!

'No!' wails Jaco. 'Mrs Morgan! Please! Not
a knife! Don't you have a pair of scissors?'

'Scissors . . .? Of course!' says Mrs
Morgan. 'That would be much easier.' She
hauls Jaco to his feet, gives him a glass of milk
to calm him down and fetches the scissors.
'Ready?'

Jaco nods. He's sorry he offered to help
now, I can tell. He closes his eyes.

Snip! Snip-snip! Snip-snip-snip!

Jaco starts to smile. He opens his eyes. 'I
can't feel it,' he says. 'It's just like having a
haircut. Oh – you won't cut it too short, will
you, Mrs Morgan?'

'No, *bach*,' she says. 'I know you boys love
your spiky hair. Like little hedgehogs, you are!
Don't you worry. I'll do a neat job. And you'll
feel better for it, you know. This is a lot of
weight to be carrying around on your head.'

Mrs Morgan is right. Jaco does feel better
afterwards. And the soup is scrummy. Mrs
Morgan lets us taste it before she gives it to

everyone else. But she makes us promise not to tell anyone what it is made from. I mean, would you fancy eating a bowl of my brother's hair?

Chapter 6

The Big Match

After lunch I get Jaco ready for the Big
Match. I swap his underpants for shorts.
Take off his trainers and tie on his football
boots. Then we go out onto the field.

It's a gorgeous day. Not a cloud in the
sky. Three coaches are pulling up outside the
school. They're here! Wood Green Juniors!
We play them every Saint David's Day.
Sometimes we win, sometimes we don't.
They always have a good team.

Mr Brangan is already on the pitch. He's
the teacher in charge of our team. He looks
Jaco up and down.

'You can't play in that, lad,' he says. 'This
is a serious game, not a charity knockabout.
Get changed quick.'

Jaco sighs and explains – for the
hundredth time today – that he isn't wearing
a costume.

Mr Brangan frowns. 'Then you can't play,' he says. 'You're so stiff. You'll have to be a goalpost, lad.'

A goalpost? Jaco stares at him in horror and so do I. Our Jaco's a striker. One of the best there is.

'I can't be a goalpost,' Jaco wails. 'It's true – I am too stiff to bend. But I can run really fast.'

'You can't turn your head,' says Mr Brangan. 'How will you see the ball? No, Jaco, I'm sorry. You're out of the team.'

'But I've trained so hard,' says Jaco. There are tears in his eyes now. 'It's such a special game. I really want us to beat them.'

'And we *shall* beat them,' says Mr Brangan confidently.

'Not without me,' says Jaco. 'You need me. I've scored more goals than anyone else this season.'

Mr Brangan sighs. 'Well . . .'

'Please?'

'You can be a substitute. That's the best I can do, lad. Take it or leave it.'

Jaco crumples like a wet tissue. 'I'll take it,' he says in a tiny voice, and he shuffles off to the side of the pitch.

Chapter 7

Go Jaco!

Out come the teams. Our boys get a massive cheer. The whole school is watching, infants and juniors. The Wood Green lads have brought big support too. They won't be easy to beat – not without Jaco.

The referee steps forward. He's one of the football coaches from the local leisure centre. He blows his whistle – *fffeeeeee!* – and that's it! Game on!

Jaco starts leaping up and down like a pogo stick. He's shouting, pointing, telling everyone what to do. It's one of the best games I have ever seen – fast, furious and full of rough stuff. But no goals. The teams are too well-matched.

Ffffeeeee! It's half-time. The teams huddle together. Two girls from Class 6 take them cut-up oranges. The lads suck on them like vegetarian vampires. The oranges, I mean –

not the girls. Then the whistle blows and the game carries on.

But now it's getting *really* rough. People want to win and it's not happening. There is pushing and pulling. Wild kicks. Late tackles and – *ffffeeeeee!*

Ryan Blake crashes to the ground, brought down by the Wood Green Number 7.

'Foul!' shouts Jaco. 'Send him off, Ref!'

But the ref isn't listening. He's trying to control the players. There's a fight breaking out on the pitch. Mr Brangan is there, but he's too busy looking at Ryan Blake's leg. It's badly cut. We can see the blood from here. Brilliant!

Now Mr Brangan is helping Ryan off. 'You're on, Evans,' he shouts.

'Yes, sir!' cries Jaco. He scuttles onto the pitch like a crab. The Wood Green lads stop fighting and stare at him. They can't believe what they are seeing. They grin, snigger, laugh in his face. But not for long, because the whistle blows and the game is back on.

Glyn Carter passes Jaco the ball. 'Go,

Jaco!' I yell. He starts to run, but the Wood Green Number 7 shoves him from behind. *Doomf!* Jaco has no chance. He smashes facedown into the ground.

'Foul!' I shout. 'Ref! Send him off!'

A couple of our boys haul Jaco to his feet. He's covered in mud.

'Ooh!' says the Number 7. 'I do like a bit of gravy on my leeks!'

Ffffeeee!

That's it! The Ref has had enough of Wood Green Number 7. He's sending him off! *Ye-e-e-e-s!* I'm jumping up and down like my bum's on fire. Now they are down to ten men. We can do this. We can beat them. *Come on, Jaco!*

The game begins again. The sun is still beating down and the teams are working harder than ever. I can see the sweat on their faces. Their shirts are sticking to their backs. Jaco must be boiling but he doesn't seem to care. He's got the ball again and he's making a run for goal.

Down the pitch he goes – and no one

tackles him. What's going on? The Wood Green lads want to stop him. You can see it in their eyes. But as soon as they get close, their faces pucker in disgust. It's the stink, coming off our Jaco! Great pongy waves – enough to turn anyone's stomach. No one dares go close.

Jaco is running like a centipede. He's past the last of the defenders. Now there is only him and the goalkeeper. The goalie doesn't know what to do. The smell is punching him in the face. He's starting to turn green. He's crying. He desperately wants to run away. But he's a goalie. He can't leave the goal wide open. Can he?

You bet he can! Suddenly the goalie is off, heading for the toilets. Run, boy, run!

So now Jaco has an open goal. He slows down, takes aim and shoots –

'GOAL!!' The whole school shouts as one. It's so loud, they must hear it in Cardiff. And now everyone is up and dancing. Mr Brangan grabs hold of Mrs Williams and spins her round. She giggles like an auntie at a wedding.

The ref blows his whistle and calls everyone

back to order. The game begins again, but we think it's all over.

Fffffeeeeeeee! It is now!

We swarm onto the pitch. Jaco is lifted into the air and carried like a Christmas tree, round and round until everyone has seen him. Finally he ends up in front of Mrs Williams. The lads put him down and he stands there, grinning from ear to ear.

'Jac Evans,' says Mrs Williams. 'You have been a real hero today.'

Today? *Pah!* That's nothing. Jaco is my hero *every* day!

Chapter 8

Tingles in the Dark

So now it is ten o'clock and we're lying in our beds, back where it all began.

'I'm so-o-o-o tired,' I say. I'm yawning like next door's dog. 'You must be worn out too.'

'Mmm,' sighs Jaco. 'But I'm glad I did it.'

'I hope you can change back. Do you think you'll be a boy by morning?'

'By midnight, I think. I can feel it wearing off already. I've got tingles all over my body.'

'I'm glad,' I say. 'It's been a right laugh, but it's been hard work. Looking after you, picking you up . . .'

'Sorry,' says Jaco sleepily. 'I'll try to make it easier for you next year.'

'Next year?!' I leap up in bed, wide-awake now. 'You're not going to be a leek *again*, are you?'

'Nah,' says Jaco. 'Next year I'm going to be a dragon.'

And though it's too dark
to see him, I know he's
grinning.

Meet the Author

Shall I make him flesh and blood?

Or stone . . .

or bone . . .

or wax . . .

or wood?

I'm not surprised the main character in this book is a vegetable! I never seem to write about flesh and blood heroes. My first two novels were about wooden children; my third featured a werewolf and a girl who turned into a fox, and I've just started writing a story about a man made entirely of marmalade!

I love the art of shape-shifting. It's so magical – and very inspiring. If your hero isn't fleshy but made of something else instead, your story will have endless plot possibilities. Try it and see!

Find out more about Cat at
www.catweatherill.co.uk

Jaco the leek

'Look out, world! Here comes JACO THE LEEK!'

Jaco Evans is tired of dressing up for the Saint David's Day celebrations in school. So he makes a wish – and turns into Leek Boy!

How will Jaco get his pants on when he has no legs? Will the school cook chop him up for lunch? Will he get to play against Wood Green Juniors in the annual Saint David's Day football match?

Fast and funny and ever so stinky... This is one Saint David's Day he'll never forget!

www.pontbooks.co.uk

ISBN 978-1-84323-913-0

9 781843 239130

Pont £4.99

Cover illustration: Brett Breckon